The Party Was Over

Imi Books
PO Box 11, Mapo Post Office
Mapo-daero 89, Mapo-gu
Seoul 04156, Korea

imibooks@nate.com
ymchoi30@hotmail.com

The Party Was Over
POEMS : written by Choi Young-Mi
/ translated by Alice Kim and Seung-Hee Jeon.
p. cm.

ISBN 979-11-967142-1-5 (03810)

Cover and text design by Yeo Hyun-mi
/edited by Kim Sora
Photograph of Choi Young-Mi by Jung, Hakyung

The Party Was Over

/ Poems /

Choi Young-Mi

Translated by Alice Kim
and Seung-Hee Jeon

Imi Books

CONTENTS

I

II

III

I

For those
who have never been young,
hence never can age

Already

Shoes already wet
Don't get wet again

A person already sad
Doesn't cry

Those who already have
Don't hurt

A body already in pain
Doesn't suffer shame

Things already hot
Don't say a word

At Thirty, The Party Was Over

Of course I know, that I liked
the revolutionist rather than the revolution,
the bar rather than the drinks.
And when I was lonely,
I've enjoyed the sweet hum of a love song
rather than an "O Comrades!" anthems.
But does it matter now?

The party is over.
The liquor's gone,
and though people left one by one,
finally even he;
after paying their dues,
and finding their shoes.

I know, in the back of my mind
that
there will be somebody here, alone,

cleaning up the table,

remembering everything with her bitter tears,

that

she will finish the unfinished song that he had started.

Yes, maybe, I know

that

she will set up the table and call them

back

before the sunrise.

She will light the stage once more

with all preparations done.

But does it matter now?

Monster

Don't sit next to Mr. En

the poet K warned me, new to the literary world

because if he's near a young woman, he'll touch her

I forgot K's warning and sat next to Mr. En–

Me too–

the silk jacket borrowed from my sister got rumpled

Years later, at a publisher's new year party

I saw En grope the married editor sitting next to me and

I shouted

"You slimy old man!"

slamming into a poet thirty years my senior as I fled

if En threw something at me, a beer glass

it would ruin my new black vest

so I left the restaurant in Mapo,

my coat hem fluttering behind me

His 100 volumes of poetry –
"En is a faucet. Just turn it and, water gushes out
but it's sewage water!"
Even Park the novelist who lambasted him
(when it was just us)
kept quiet as En's body grew into a monster

They don't even know that the water they drink is sewage
the poor public

Each time En's name is discussed as a Notul Prize candidate
I think if En really wins the Notul Prize
I have to quit this country
I don't want to live in this filthy society

Now that we have raised a monster –
How do we catch the monster?

At the Fruit Stand

Apples do not know Peaches

Peaches do not know Grapes

Grapes do not know those sour Tangerines

All of you from different places, yet

one fall afternoon,

leaning so easy on each other's back, like married couples

pushing and pulling,

turning red and blue,

This world is becoming beautiful.

Song of March

Ever changing blooming magnolia
oblivious to why it must bloom
while pushing away winter
leaf becomes flower.

Even before your broad hand
touches me, I burst
while I dance on your palm and
turn on music to muffle the moans⋯

Stop.
Even the sun cools eventually.

Our white magnolia
throws up
what will not come again.

Old

1. Spring Day
For forsythia to bloom
one warm day is enough,
will spring come for me too?

2. At East Seoul Terminal
Sating my hunger with a cold sandwich
I bit into an old emptiness

3. Poetry Class
When teaching poetry
I could not write a line of my own

4. One AM
A twinkling cross in a hazy sky
where are those children
I have thrown away?

5. Traffic Accident

Things that spin quickly are invisible

when watching all of you race thrillingly

lying below the blue sky…

6. Saturday Afternoon

Ordering stuff and running the vacuum

while eating and talking and smoking

lips that burn away the nothingness

stretched out from 55 years of opening and shutting

Have you ever smelled the stench of rotting beauty?

The stronger the odor, the more tragic it is

7. An Old Diary

I have not left this land that tires me

I have not escaped this literary neighborhood that stifles me

I have not yet thrown out my family

The Aftertaste Is Not Bitter

Oldest in the morning,
in the evening, grown young again.

When the dark blankets the night with an eyelid,
I become a young, young child
and climb the little hill from long ago,
fumbling where my dream used to be.

Wandering, looking for raspberries,
I wasn't afraid,
didn't hear my mother nagging, Why are you late?
or the noise of the clock.

I come down from the hill, my old playground,
and even after waking from my dream,
living and eating my cowardly meals,
I believe, somewhere, the aftertaste is not bitter,
my share of sweet raspberries remain for me,

in hiding with a twinkling eye.

An innocent purity
has preserved this world.

My 50s

Scarier than an ex-lover are the stairs

Even to come down from the 2nd floor⋯
An elevator?
If there are no empty seats on the bus on rainy days
I regret going out to the museum
I'm done with art, everything's a hassle
I become a stretched out piece of meat
If I wobble while holding on to the strap
My whole life wobbles too

If I hadn't turned it down⋯

A comfortable seat is more welcome than a best friend
And when my gums hurt, I don't want to live

Novel, Postscript

Gotta write, gotta write, can't write,

to Europe, to America, to Chuncheon,

dragging the heavy bundle of the novel behind me,

switching my unused notebook twice,

replacing a blameless keyboard three times,

letting 10 fruitless years drain away.

That evening,

after you appeared in front of me like a novel,

in the heart of bubbling, boiling winter,

the sentences came bouncing. Even painlessly.

II

Don't give that which is holy to the dogs,

neither throw your pearls before the pigs···

— Matthew 7: 6

To The Pigs

On an afternoon when I was really exhausted,
I gave a pearl to a pig.

Jumping up and down with joy, he ran to the other pigs
And bragged that he got to own my pearl.
But it was a cracked pearl.
He doesn't know
In my drawer, clearer flawless pearls are sleeping…
In my house on a deserted beach on a lonely island,
Deep inside my wardrobe that I haven't shown anybody,
Pearls that change their colors according to the weather,
Pearls that resemble the mystery of the sea where I was born,
About a thousand of them are waiting to be strung…

People don't know that
The pearl he has
Is an ugly pearl that can't even be sold at the market.
I don't care if it becomes a children's toy.

I don't care if talkative pigs chew it while drinking.

I forgot when and where,
In a hut I entered for shelter from the rain,
I gave a pearl
To a pig I happened to meet.
(It's not important what his name was)
Because it was so pitch dark,
I didn't know he was a pig.
I didn't want to know who he was.
I only vaguely realized that my pocket was picked.

Since that day, ten pigs ganged up on me
And shouted and asked for a pearl.
When I pretended not to hear,
They waited at my street corner.
And after making sure nobody was around
Knocked at the door of my house.

"Give me a pearl.

You have to give me one too.

You must!"

They began with a polite request,

But ended with a shameless demand.

Simply too tired, reluctantly,

And because I was afraid their cry would wake up my neighbors,

I gave a pearl to an unfamiliar pig.

(It was an even uglier pearl)

The next morning, even before the sun rose,

Twenty fat pigs appeared at the door of my house.

Together with wolves and foxes,

Those ferocious animals climbed the wall,

Trampled on the flowerbed in the yard, overturned flower pots,

Broke delicate branches of my touch-me-nots.

Some shamelessly

Sang and danced in the flower bed I couldn't guard.

Then, strong pigs broke the door and entered the kitchen

And ate my bread and drank the wine I had saved for a rainy day.

Squeezing out the last sweet drop, their party went on.

Young wolves were cruel,

And old foxes, knowing the way of the world, were cunning.

In order to guard my precious treasures,

I fought and bled.

Sometimes I fought, other times I compromised.

When they asked for two, I gave one,

Sometimes I deceived them with a fake pearl necklace.

But they didn't retreat.

I ran away.

I ran far, far away to where they couldn't follow me.

I borrowed money from friends and traveled by train and ship.

I tore up the letters they sent, and I hung up on their calls.

Still those greedy pigs wouldn't give up.

Returning from a long trip,

I'm now old and sick.

I don't even have the strength to get up, but

They ask me for a pearl,

A pearl just one last time⋯

In Sun-woon Temple

Flowers,
How slow to open into flowers
How quick to fall –

Not enough time to look at all
Not enough time to think of you, my love
Just a moment to fall –

Just like
The First time you blossomed in my heart
I wish just for that moment to forget you

Your face, smiling far away
Your face, slipping over the mountains

Flowers,
so quick to fall –
But it takes too long to forget
Forever to forget.

11 O'clock Sunday Morning

God, dumped by Europeans,

Picked up by a stubby Asian hand,

Thrust into a speaker

In the Subway 4

Three women are dozing,
one woman's head on another's shoulder,
one woman's shoulder on another's chest,
one woman's weariness on yet another's worries,
do re mi, one two three.

Three men are approaching,
the subway like the innards of a sausage,
pushing past the poached, browbeaten eyeballs,
climbing over the boiled, slack flesh.

First a beggar holds out a hand,
next a blind man sings a song,
then a prophet with a bushy head of hair:
"People of the world, prepare for the end!"
hollering and waking the crowd, he wanders, but

three women are dozing,

three men are approaching,

11 in the morning, the subway is
stuffed with the jobless.

In the Subway 5

His bottom and

My bosom lean and make a wall together,

His newspaper and

My novel quiver in unison,

His unease and

My dissatisfaction taunt each other in turns,

His yawns and

My sighs unlatch mouths, side by side,

His black noodle and

My bibimbap criss-cross, growling.

His loneliness and

My isolation straighten our collars,

No one says a word on the subway at 8 am.

His watch and

My watch both get in line,

His living and

My life blunder when they meet.
Slowly, we age.

His Buddha and
My God gaze down on this world –
Oh humanity!
*Om mani padme hum**

---

* the bodhisattva of compassion
  "the lord who gazes down on this world"

In the Subway: Yellow October

October Revolution

Yellow October is Coming, Tiburon TGX
Fastest in the Country, the Birth of a More
Progressive Sports Car

Revolution now exists only in an advertisement.

The ten dancing characters are stirring up a storm in your heart,

When you are stealing a glance at the newspaper beside you.

Confronting the speed of only dashing and looking forward,

You would rather blow yourself up.

Children are playing in front of you, shooting toy guns.

Stirring up yellow dust, yellow revolution

Attacks you on the front page of the newspaper.

Pierced by a sharp autumn sunray

Flying into the train across the windowsill,

I close my eyes

And snow-covered Russia is soaked in blood in October.

Until red October became yellow October,

Until Lenin's face is overlapping with a Hyundai car,

What have we been doing?

Yellow October, amazing October, is rushing in.

Buy me, turn-of-the-century capitalism!

Wake me up from my long sleep,

Spanning from red October to yellow October,

Please shake me up –

the lowest-speed-in-the-country engine is attached to me.

Lying lips never go dry,

I feel like indicting them, but there's no court.

Scattered, each and every broken rock remains silent.

Seoul, June 2008

Old photos, blood-smeared newspaper clippings

Hanging on the wall in the square,

And the songs ringing out of speakers,

Wow! They are the same songs

That we heard twenty years ago,

But the leaflets they leisurely hand out in the road

Are printed better on thicker paper.

Printed in the IT powerhouse of the twenty-first century,

The red exclamation marks look elegant,

And the faces of those gathered,

Aren't distorted by rage,

Unlike in the 1980s

When we protested against the military dictatorship.

Lights in their eyes are as gentle as candle light

Burning safely within the paper cups they are holding,

Their healthy lips don't risk their lives,

They don't know slogans they would shout and die for.

Unable to stand arms bumping into my shoulders,
I handed my candle to a young man next to me
And went to the underground.

How handsome the young man escorting women and
babies in the square!
The breed of Korean men brilliantly improved.
History progresses like this, you know.

Chattering with a friend in an Italian restaurant,
I slashed raw salmon meat with a knife.
Without holding the foam of a guilty
Feeling in my mouth…

III

A bird calls me:

Let us meet again on this lonely planet

Weather Forecasts

Warm air from the south,
Cold air from the north,
And torrential rain advisories.

You were cold.
I was hot.
And men I met
In order to forget you
Were tepid–
Neither cold nor hot.

Dangerous typhoons of my life are over.
Poems, having survived, are printed on paper,
And cars are moving sluggishly.

Tomorrow will be cloudy,
And I will go out
To buy a bottle of shampoo.

On My Way to the Department Store

Half of my desire
Is satisfied in the department store.

Groceries are in the basement
Cosmetics on the first floor
Jeans on the second floor
Shoes on the third floor
Bed···

The whole world gathers here.
Believing that he will satisfy
The remaining half of my desire
That's not on display
Even in department stores in America and Europe,
I have waited ten years, twenty years.

You aren't here yet, though.

Waiting for him

In order to be found by him,

I collect fatal fragrances.

Chanel, Dior, Aveda…

An uneasy afternoon during which I can't buy anything,

Because I want to have,

Because I don't want to have,

Shampoo's on the first floor

Jeans on the second floor

Shoes on the third floor,

Where is he?

Where is he going now?

Dreams of Four Seasons

Some dreams don't grow old,
They simply congeal on the windowsill.
My wish to run beside him either on land or in the sea
Hasn't been fulfilled.

Some dreams were so stupid,
I couldn't wake up from hibernation
Even when spring and summer came.

Some dreams were so private,
I couldn't take them out of my pocket.

Some dreams were so sweet,
They melted as soon as they touched my tongue
Like ice cream on a summer day.

Some dreams grew old so quickly.
I forgot what I gave up, before the fall breezes arrived.

Some dreams were so fragile,

Flared up and died like cigarette smoke

Without inscribing their names in winter trees.

I don't hold onto wishes that can't be fulfilled.

I'm afraid of falling asleep

And of waking up,

But petals still fall whenever seasons change,

Even if I cannot fix dreams of spring days in the fall⋯

At Home All Day

I lift
The faucet handle

Up
Down
Up
Down

Brush my teeth
Wash my body
Wash the dishes
Clean the floor

I lift
The faucet handle

Up and down
Up and down···

One tattered evening,

A toothless old woman will be peering into a mirror.

Through the hole where desire has passed

A breeze will blow in and out.

The Easiest Path

I used to close my eyes,

In bed
On the sofa
In the car
In the tent
On the dirty ground
Lying on a warm boulder

In the flowing river
In the stagnant water
In the soapsuds of the bath
Under the chilly blanket

To search for a happiness that doesn't exist,
I closed my eyes.

Now,

At the kitchen table

With my eyes wide open,

The pleasures that visit every day

I smash into fragments

And push through a hole

Lips smudged with the blood of fresh meat.

Under the Name of Woman

Not me but us

Not you but us

Let's say us, even if we don't want to.

In this life we have swept and cleaned and nourished,

we had to sit at the very back.

The things we swept and cleaned and nourished,

though they betray us,

we had to endure it.

That I must endure,

is what my mother taught me.

Those who we fed and washed and put to bed,

while waiting for them to return,

we put on the armor of obedience and duty,

with words we could not spit out in words.

Destroyed dreams.

The silence of a thousand years.

Under the name of mother,
of wife,
we become a slave or a doll.

Unless he, unless they, abandoned us,
we could not abandon them.
Unless they left us, we had no freedom to leave.
Not only long ago, but even now,
all over the globe,
these things happen to young girls.

Not mother,
not wife,
but under the name of woman we must write our history.

 Not mother, not wife,

but with the eyes of woman let's look at the world,

so we can see this crooked world straight.

All the trembling voices come outside,

united voices join to become a battle cry that destroys a wall.

Overcome fear

with the miracle of me becoming we.

Not sparkling like a jewel,

but a star in each other's hearts.

Irony

There was a time when I begged
for the rain to never stop⋯

Another time I begged again,
please, please, for the rain to stop⋯

At one time, at another time,
on rainy nights, I would knead out a song,
I massaged the suffering of my days,
to draw out a metaphor's tune.

If only this rain would never stop...
Please, please, if only this rain would stop⋯

Folding Towels

I can't fix this wreck of a world with my own hands,

But I can fold a towel however I want.

I love the organization of my cabinet and drawers.

If I remember to bring in the laundry on Sunday afternoons,

Life seems to glide.

I fold the underwear I need to endure another week.

As they pass through my hands, clothing of every shape

Turns into a small square.

This dirty world,

While my will to fight ignites, I fold a towel.

If I can put on clean underwear every day,

I'm ready to face anyone.

The day I grow tired of folding laundry is the day

I might as well, without regret,

Leave this land that has only shown me dirtiness,

Hazy sky, eyes so violated by tear gas and particulate dust,
Clear days bring on tears.

On a rare, radiant spring day,
I roll the towels lengthwise, the way I learned from him,
Line them up in the cabinet, the overlapping memories.
It has already been twenty years,
But you are my young man forever
(I never introduced him to my mother).

After parting from you, I only wore white.
He never liked my saggy underwear,
Teased me that I was like a granny.
Mine are white.
Mom's are yellowed.
When they were dry, I picked out the white towels,
The yellowed towels fell on the floor.
I'm sorry, Mom.

Mom doesn't fold towels anymore,

She can't even wash her hair by herself.

She waits all week for Saturday, the day I give her a bath,

I complain that Saturday comes too quickly.

Before I pack my mother's faded underwear in a bag,

I check them for smells.

Tainting no one,

Like a lettuce leaf wrapped around savage meat,

You have lived so sweetly,

But shrink as the days pass.

Even the best washing machine can't lift the smell of death.

I don't like my towels to mix with Mom's towels,

My fussiness about hygiene is from her.

I seal her germs in a plastic bag,

And turn at the sound of an explosion –

Like the flash of a missile striking Syria –

Tearing apart the gloom –

Splitting my chest in two –

Long-buried words burst forth from me⋯

I can't fix this disaster of a world,

But I love the organization of the comma, and the periods.

About myself

Let me tell you a story about dreams from my father. My childhood memory begins with my father, talking in his sleep almost every night.

"Kill them all! Uoo·····Ah····aha···Shoot!"

My father who accidently killed his soldier during the Korean war, had a lot of horrible memories. My mother told me much later that he would stop sleep-talking, only when he had love affairs. He was a playboy all through his life.

Now I think his sleep-talking is very poetic. Uoo···Ah···aha··· it might breed my imagination.

"What is he talking about?"

" Why he should kill people every night?"

A little girl wondered at her bed.

My father was connected to many important political upheavals in modern Korean history. When he was in his high school, he carried a grenade in his pocket to assassinate the famous leftist leader, Yu Oon-hyung(여운형). He cried when he heard the news that Yu was killed by another terrorist. (He wanted the glory for himself.)

I have been accustomed to sudden disappear of father. He would be held in custody whenever American presidents visited Korea. My mother hid him in the closet when Johnson visited. My father remains a naive right wing liberalist. We remained in poverty as he came in and out of prison several times.

I grew up in an era of anxiety, under my anxious father, fed on his anxious meals. I turned to reading books to kill that anxiety, before the anxiety kills me. Literature was my destiny.

In 1980, when I was a freshman at Seoul national university, the center of Student Movement, Gwang-ju massacre happened. My collage shut down, and my youth shut down as well. Unlike my father, I was a thinker rather than activist. I joined the demonstration neither in front of the barricade nor in the back with my arms crossed.

I always hesitated at the crucial moment. I was one of a underground group of translators of Marxist texts. I fought with foreign languages, instead of fighting directly military dictatorship.

In 1992 after the Soviet collapsed, I made my literary debuts. I choose to remain an outsider from Korean literary circles. I think I am as vulnerable as a soft tofu. But when my freedom is challenged, I stand up, ready to fight.

Acknowledgments

The following five poems were first translated by Seung-Hee Jeon for *AZALEA* (Journal of Korean Literature & Culture, Volume six, Korea Institute Harvard University 2013) : "11 O'clock Sunday Morning" "To the Pigs" "Dreams of Four Seasons" "In the Subway: Yellow October" and "Seoul, June 2008". Jeon also translated "Weather Forecasts" and "On My Way to the Department Store" for *Asia, Magazine of Asian Literature* (Seoul: 2011)

Alice Kim is the translator of "Monster" "Old" "Novel, Postscript" "My 50s" "In the Subway 4" "In the Subway 5" "The Aftertaste Is Not Bitter" "At Home All Day" "The Easiest Path" "Already" "Song of March" "Under the Name of Woman" "Irony" "Folding Towels"

Several people were involved in the translations of "At the Fruit Stand" "In Sun-woon Temple" and "At Thirty, The Party Was Over".

*

Seung-Hee Jeon and Alice Kim have my deepest gratitude for their passionate efforts in translating my poems. Some of the poems selected from my 6 volumes of poetry, and presented here are in slightly different forms from when these translations first appeared.

I am deeply grateful to James Kimbrell, Chase Twichell, and Sarah Gorham for their support. I would like to thank my sister Young Joo Choi, my nephew Young Woo Cho, my cousin Jeong-Woo Lee and Haran Choi.

My sincere appreciation goes to Bo Seo, Hayeon Na, Kim Sora, Eugene Lee, B.K. Ju, Sunju Choi Chong, Joyce Park and everyone for helping to bring my poems to an international audience. I am especially grateful to Moon Sook, Ranhee Song, Korean Women's Hotline, Ingrid Yeh, and the 4th World Conference of Women's Shelters. Much love to all my friends and everyone in support of the #MeToo Movement.

Notes

1. "At Thirty, The Party Was Over" I found this translation from YouTube video (https://www.youtube.com/watch?v=okOY6KjqmXo) that Korean Male ASMR posted. At that video he said "I found this translation at the comment from the following site: http://www.poetrytranslation.org Now they deleted the post···"

I tried to find the translator through SNS. Anyone who knows about this translation, please let me know.

2. "In Sun-woon Temple" 'Sun-woon Temple' in Korean peninsula is famous for its flower, Camellias. The poem "In Sun-woon Temple" is about flower and love, but some Korean readers read it as a symbol of revolution.

3. "About myself" is written for 'lunch poem' On April 2009 at U.C. Berkeley.

The Author

Choi Young-Mi (최영미/崔泳美) is a poet and novelist from the Republic of Korea, and is one of the defining figures who ignited the #MeToo movement in Korea.

Born in Seoul in 1961. She received her B.A. in Western History from Seoul National University and an M.A. in Art History from Hong-ik University. Faced with the military dictatorship of 1980's, she participated in student protest demanding for democracy. As a result, she was detained at police station for 10 days and was suspended from university for a year.

Her first volume of poems *"At Thirty, the Party Was Over* (1994)"* came across as a shock to the literary world and to the Korean society thanks to her delicate but bold expressions, lively metaphor, and the piercing satire on capital and authority. *"At Thirty, the Party Was Over"* has sold over half a million copies.

She is the author of *Treading on the Pedals of Dreams* (1998), *To the Pigs* (2005, 2014), *Life that has yet to Arrive* (2009), *Things Already Hot* (2013) *and What will not come again* (2019) which includes the poem "Monster" and other #Metoo poems.

She received the Isu Literary Award for *To the Pigs* in 2006 and her fifth volume of poems, *Things Already Hot* was selected as Book Culture Foundation's Literary Book of Excellence in 2013.

In 2005 Choi wrote her first novel *Scars and Patterns* to transform as a novelist. She is the author of *Bronze Garden* and a collection of essays *Melancholy of the Era.* Choi has also translated *"Francis Bacon in Conversation with Michel Archimbaud"* (1998) and *"D'Aulaires' Book of Greek Myths"*(1999) into Korean.

In 2017, the editor of a magazine requested Choi Young-Mi to write poems on feminism and gender struggle. By accepting this request, she wrote the poem "Monster" (괴물) that exposed the sexual harassment and abuse by the old poet En. When her poem "Monster" released, the public immediately noticed that 'En' is Ko (the most revered

Korean poet), which ignited the #Me Too movement.

Choi Young-Mi's revelation of Ko's molestation has played a major role in exposing the sexual harassments and assaults infested deep inside the Korean society, not only in the cultural and arts community, and her contributions will help eradicate any further offenders. For this contribution, the Metropolitan City of Seoul has decided to present Choi Young-Mi with the grand prize of Sex Equality Award 2018.

Poet Ko sued her for defamation in summer 2018, but he has lost the case against poet Choi Young-Mi. The Seoul Central District Court (Feb. 15, 2019) sided with Choi saying her allegations of sexual harassment were credible. The court said her testimony was "consistent and specific," while there was "little reason to doubt the veracity of her claims."

The Translators

Alice Kim

Alice Kim was born in Seoul, Korea and immigrated to the United States when she was one year old. She has been a lawyer for 20 years and taught English in Korea through the Fulbright program and at Seoul National University. She holds a degree in English and Linguistics from Yale University, and a law degree from Columbia Law School. She lives in New Jersey and spends the summers in Seoul with her (very handsome) husband and two (impossibly perfect) children (who like to read over her shoulder when she is working).

Seung-Hee Jeon

Seung-Hee Jeon is a literary scholar and critic as well as a leading contemporary translator of Korean literature. Her translations include the 2016 Man Booker Prize-winning novelist Han Kang's *Convalescence* (2013) and Bang Hyeon-seok's fiction *Time to Eat Lobster* (2016), which was selected for "75 Notable Translations of the Year" by *World Literature Today* as well as *Conscience in Action: The Autobiography of Kim Dae-jung* (2018), the authoritative autobiography by the 2000 Nobel Peace Prize winner and late South Korean President Kim Dae-jung. She has been honored with a Fulbright Grant, a Korea Foundation Fellowship, and two Daesan Foundation Translation grants. Based in both Boston and Seoul, she is a visiting assistant professor in Korean at Boston College.

Reviews

"A clear language full of polysemy"

— The Asahi Shimbun

"Choi Young-mi wrote the poem in Korean, her native tongue. It is a language that tends first to cool its emotions, then to assimilate them; unruly drama and dialogue, in their retelling, take on the muted affect of melancholy."

— Bo Seo, the Paris Review

"Choi's poetry sharply stabs the Korean society's hypocrisy, fallacy and complacency and once again as the conscience of the generation she provides the raison d'être for poets."

— Jongho Yu, THE ISU LITERARY AWARD, Judge's Citation

"Her sincerity in writing poems and elaborative language stand out."

— Kyungrim Shin, Poet

How to Order

The Party Was Over

poems by Choi Young-Mi

ISBN: 979-11-967142-1-5 (03810)

You can order "The Party Was Over" on line through YES24's website‚ https://global.yes24.com/

If you have any questions, please send inquiries to the publisher :

imibooks@nate.com

ymchoi30@hotmail.com

Imi Books

PO Box 11, Mapo Post Office

Mapo-daero 89, Mapo-gu

Seoul, Korea

www.facebook.com/youngmi.choi.96155